It was Christmas Eve and David was snug and warm in his cozy bed. He was trying so hard to go to sleep. But he could hear strange noises.

It wasn't the sound of sleigh bells.
It wasn't the sound of reindeer hoofs on the roof.
It wasn't even the sound of Santa unpacking his sack.

It was more of a

HARUMPH!

and an

OOF!

It was no use.

There'd be no sleep for David
until he'd found out what
was making that noise.

David crept down the stairs and peered into the living room. There were three stockings hanging from the fireplace.

One of them belonged to David. But where had the other two come from? Suddenly, a muffled voice came from the chimney.

"Oh, dear. I'm even **more** stuck now!"

There was a scuffling sound from behind the Christmas tree, and David jumped as a small elf appeared.

"Uh, hello," said the elf. "I guess you've caught us!"

David listened as the elf explained that Santa was stuck in the chimney. The elf had tried to pull him out. But the only things that had come down so far were Santa's boots and pants!

"I can help you," suggested David. "I'll hold Santa's feet and we can both pull."
The elf agreed. "Between us, we might be able to get him unstuck."

David grasped both of Santa's feet firmly.
But, just at that moment, a light went on upstairs.
"David, is that you?" called his mom. "Back to
bed now, please, or Santa won't come!"

At that exact moment, Santa shot back up the chimney... with David still hanging onto his feet.

The poor elf could not believe his eyes.
But there was no time to think...
David's mom was coming
out of her bedroom.

"I'm coming!" squeaked the elf. He hurried
up the stairs and jumped into David's
bed, pulling the covers up over his head.
"Night-night, sweetie!" said David's
mom through the doorway.

Meanwhile, up on the roof, Santa and David had landed in a heap. The clever reindeer had hooked their reins under Santa's arms and pulled as hard as they could.

"Good job!" said Santa, brushing himself down. "No more cookies for me tonight!"

David scrambled to his feet. But Santa was so busy, he didn't notice that David and the elf had traded places!

"I think we'd better deliver the rest of the presents first," said Santa, "and leave this house for last."

Santa climbed into the driver's seat.

"Elf, you get the presents ready for our next destination," he called over his shoulder.

"But I'm not Elf..." replied David.

Santa wasn't really listening.
He was talking to the reindeer.
"Up, up, and away!" Santa called,
and the reindeer took off before
David had time to explain.

David held on tight as the
sleigh climbed high into the
night sky, above the rooftops.

Surrounded by sacks, David was so busy figuring out which presents were which, there was no time to let Santa know that there'd been a mistake.

There were big presents for the cities,

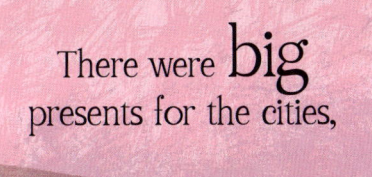

and SHINY presents for the towns.

There were ODD-shaped presents for the villages,

and mystery presents for the farms.

To David

David *shimmied* down chimneys.

He squeezed through cat flaps.

And, if all else failed, he used Santa's *magic* key to let himself in.

In each house, David picked up the cookies to take home to Mrs. Claus, and carrots for the reindeer.

Finally, there was just one sack left, and Santa still hadn't realized his mistake! The sleigh headed back over the rooftops to David's house.

David had never had so much fun as when he slid down his own chimney with a sack of his own presents.

He put his presents under the Christmas tree, then picked up Santa's pants and boots and put them in the sack.

"Psst! Elf, where are you?" whispered David.

A very happy Elf appeared, rubbing his eyes. "I've had such a lovely nap," he said. David handed over the sack and waved as Elf disappeared up the chimney.

Back in his cozy bed, David listened to the sounds of reindeer hoofs on the roof, sleigh bells, and, very faintly,

"Ho ho ho!
Merry Christmas!"

Or was that,

"Ho ho ho!
yummy cookies!"?

Write your name on the gift tags.

Draw yourself as an elf.

Create one-of-a-kind books for any child on Put Me In The Story!

visit → www.putmeinthestory.com/morenames

- Find *Unique Gifts* for birthdays, holidays, or any day
- Personalize this and other great stories with *Any Child's Name*
- Choose from over *100 Personalized* versions of bestselling children's books

www.putmeinthestory.com/morenames